the
CLOUD KIDS
THE UNTAMED DRAGON

By

Evie Chambers

To my creative, adventurous and inspiring Cloud Kids.
Love you all!

TABLE OF CONTENTS

CHAPTER ONE

Finn was in the front yard drawing a plane with his new chalk. He used yellow for the propellers, blue for the wings, and purple for the wheels down below.

He wanted it to look like a colorful version of the plane his pilot dad flew.

He colored a little bit here and a little bit there. Perfect.

Then suddenly, Rudy, one of his brothers, darted across the yard, jumped across the plane drawing, and smudged one of the wings with his foot.

Finn stared at him angrily. He was about to yell when their youngest brother, Jay, stomped barefoot toward them with his arms outstretched, fingers curled like talons, and teeth bared.

"RAWWWRRR!"

Rudy leaped behind Finn and clung onto his T-shirt. "Help, Finn, it's a d-d-dragon!"

Finn pointed at his artwork. "It took me forever to draw this and you smudged it!

"Sorry." Rudy looked at the ruined wing. "I can help fix it."

Finn shook his head and held up his blue chalk. "It's okay. I'll do it myself."

"Finn, let's play." Jay looked up at his big brother.

"RAAAAWWWWRRRR!"

Rudy hopped over the chalk plane again, and ran across the yard shouting, "Help! Dragon! Aaargh!"

Finn chuckled. He couldn't stay mad at his brothers for long. He placed the chalk in his pockets and chased after them.

He raised his arms above his head and stood on tiptoes. "RAAAAAAWWWRR! I'm a scary dragon, and I'm going to gobble you both up."

Jay ran across the yard with Rudy. They charged past the flower beds, twisted around the leafy tree, then circled the plane drawing.

Finn growled and bellowed, taking his role as a scary dragon very seriously.

As he was about to jump out and tickle his brothers, the sky let out a thunderous rumble. Hundreds of squishy dark clouds formed above them. Then giant droplets splattered down.

Finn, Rudy, and Jay rushed inside just before the downpour began. They watched the storm through the window.

Jay balanced on Finn's feet to make him tall enough to look out the window. He *oohed* and *aahed* as he watched giant raindrops fall, and flashes of bright green lightning light up the sky. He'd never seen a storm like this before!

Rudy made sure the stickers on his T-shirt hadn't fallen off in his hurry. He patted them to keep them in place: a yellow dragon, a wonky mountain, and a miniature plane.

Finn scratched his forehead and twitched his nose. Normally, he would have found a storm like this amazing. But he had spent all morning drawing his chalk plane. He wanted to show it to his dad when he returned from work. But now, he'd have to start it all over again.

As quickly as it started, the giant raindrops and green lightning stopped, followed by the sun peeking through the clouds.

Rudy and Jay rushed toward the door. They longed to get outside and hunt for puddles.

Finn shuffled outside with his head down, feeling sad about his ruined drawing.

He heard Jay say, "No way!", causing him to look up. That's when he saw it — the drawing was gone, but something else had replaced it. Something bigger than they were.

He couldn't believe it. There, in front of him, was an actual, colorful, life-sized plane!

CHAPTER TWO

Finn rubbed his eyes, convinced he must be dreaming. Rudy prodded the plane with his fingertip to check if it was real. Jay excitedly clapped his hands together.

"It's real!" Finn exclaimed. "It's the same as my drawing!"

The propellers were yellow, the wings were blue, and the wheels were purple.

There was even a smudge on the wing, identical to the one Rudy had made on the chalk drawing. All three boys peered through the window.

"One. Two. Three seats," Rudy counted with his finger.

Finn grinned. "One for each of us."

Rudy climbed in first, followed by Jay, after a boost up from Finn. The seats were comfy and soft.

Finn wriggled into the pilot's seat. He'd never been in one before. But as he looked at the controls, he realized something. He knew exactly how to fly it.

He made sure they were all fastened in. Then he leaned forward and pressed a shiny blue button.

The plane vibrated. Leaves and twigs blew past the windows. The plane rose off the ground and went *up, up, up!*

They stared out the window at the magical clouds.

Rudy pointed at one. "Wow, it looks like a fluffy bunny face."

Finn steered the plane through another one. "It looks like a giant apple."

Then they zoomed around a cloud shaped like an ice cream cone. Jay licked his lips. They flew past lots of fluffy, different-shaped clouds: a cat face with wavy whiskers, a smiling teddy bear, a zoomy race car.

"Look! There's a cloud mountain." Rudy pointed at a giant, purple and brown splotchy object. Finn squinted to get a better look at the funny-shaped cloud. It didn't look fluffy like the other ones. The closer they got to it, the bigger and rockier it looked.

It wasn't a cloud at all. It was a real mountain. And they were flying straight toward it!

Rudy closed his eyes and pressed a hand over his stickers. Jay started hiccupping nervously. Luckily, Finn stayed calm and in control of the plane. With a sharp turn to the right, he swerved, missing the mountain by inches.

Rudy opened his eyes and clapped in relief. Jay giggled through his hiccups. Finn smiled to himself.

He landed the plane on a green hill. The clouds hovered above them, in funny and fantastic shapes. They had flown to a magical land far, far away from home.

Most curious of all was the mountain now ahead of them.

CHAPTER THREE

Finn opened the plane door and took a deep breath of the chilly, crisp air. Wherever this land was, it was a lot colder than back home.

Jay—who was being impatient—scrambled across Finn's lap and out the open door. He stepped onto the ground, giggling as his bare feet touched the long, silky grass. He then ran over to a bunch of flowers and bent to inspect them.

"Jay, don't touch anything," Finn called. "We don't know if it's safe or not."

"Look!" Jay pointed at a stripy flower.

Finn hopped out of the plane and walked over to him. The coldness gave him goose bumps. His teeth chattered as he reached Jay and peered down at the stripy flower.

The brothers giggled—these flowers were very cool!

Before they could inspect anymore, a loud clatter came from the plane. Both of them ran across the grass to see what was going on.

Rudy popped his head out of the open door and threw something into Finn's arms. It was a long cape made out of the shiniest bluish-black feathers he had ever seen.

"I found them here in this chest," Rudy said, his words fading as he leaned into the back of the plane. "There's a cape for us all, and helmets, too."

Finn peered inside the plane and saw that Rudy was right. In the space behind their seats was a large wooden chest with brass handles. He was sure that hadn't been there before. But it was cold in this land and the cape felt warm and cozy.

The helmets looked like giant acorn shells with a stalk on top. Each of the boys put on their feathery capes and helmets. Finn and Rudy laughed at each other; these outfits were silly!

Jay gently rubbed his feathery cape and beamed. He felt like a magical bird in it. He spread his arms, made chirping sounds, and ran, pretending to fly off across the meadow. Despite being so small, he was incredibly fast.

"Jay, wait!" Finn called.

Jay stopped by a red bush and waved his brothers over. They exchanged looks and then hurried to meet him. As Jay waited, he wiggled a finger in front of the bush.

Finn shouted over to him, "Don't touch anything!"

Jay moved away from the bush and crouched to inspect a purple bug with a glittery shell.

Out of the sky came an echoing *ROARRRRRR!* It was so loud it caused the ground to tremble.

Finn and Rudy grabbed onto each other's arms so that they didn't fall over.

Jay fell onto his bottom and peered up at the sky. There was another, even louder ROARRRRR!

Then a shiny, yellow-scaled creature zoomed above them. It was a small dragon. Finn and Rudy ducked into the grass. The dragon flew past them and moved toward Jay.

"Jay, stay down!" Finn shouted.

Jay looked up, and with a big smile on his face, he waved at the creature. There was a flash of yellow as the dragon swooped down, grasping Jay in its talons and flying off with him.

Finn and Rudy ran after Jay. They leaped into the air to try to grab him, but it was no use. The dragon flew across the land with their brother tightly clutched in its talons, with Jay waving goodbye as they disappeared in the distance.

CHAPTER FOUR

Finn and Rudy didn't know what to do. A small dragon had flown off with their brother! Now, they had no idea how to get him back.

"Don't worry, Jay, we'll find you!" Finn shouted to the sky.

"We're coming, Jay," Rudy added.

The trouble was they didn't know where the dragon had taken Jay. Or how they were meant to find him.

"What now?" Rudy asked.

"The dragon flew in that direction." Finn pointed toward the mountain. "So, let's go this way."

The boys marched across the rolling green hills, through shadowy dense forests, and past a snaking river that was pink and looked like melting strawberry ice cream. Upon sniffing the river and sticking a finger in it, Rudy realized that it tasted just like strawberry ice cream, too. Both boys ate some—it was delicious!

"I hope the dragon gives Jay ice cream." Rudy licked his sticky fingers.

Finn shook his head. "I don't think dragons eat ice cream."

"Then what do they eat?"

"Hmm, not sure. I think they like fish. But I don't know if there will be any fish in an ice cream river."

"But Jay only likes fish sticks," Rudy said with concern. "Do you think the dragon will have those?"

Finn replied, "I don't think so."

Rudy didn't like the thought of his little brother being hungry. Or worse, being made to eat yucky, slimy fish.

"I'm sure Jay will be fine. He probably has pockets full of candy."

Rudy nodded and managed a faint smile. Finn was right,

Jay often snuck candy, cereal, or pieces of fruit in his pockets.

They continued on their way. They stomped through the long, silky grass and called Jay's name. As Finn took a step forward, the grass gave way beneath his feet and he fell with a *whoosh*.

Rudy was confused. His brother had been right there next to him, but now he'd vanished.

"Finn, where are you?" he shouted.

"Down here," a voice grumbled from below him. "Try not to fall in, too."

Rudy took small steps across the grass and found a hole. He knelt and peered into it. He spotted Finn in a pit full of thick slime.

Rudy wrinkled his nose. "Ew! That's so smelly."

"It's gooey, too." Finn wiped some of the gloop off his face. "Help me get out of here."

Rudy tried lowering his arm to reach Finn, but the hole was too deep. He needed something longer, so he left Finn and went looking for something to use.

He was searching around a tree when he heard rustling.

He bravely asked, "Um… h-hello. Is s-someone there?"

A girl stepped out in front of him. She was wearing the same feathered cape and acorn shell helmet as he was. Her long, red hair tumbled in waves down the shiny feathers.

She pointed at his cape and asked, "What dragon-tamer clan do you belong to?"

Rudy looked confused. He'd never heard of dragon tamers before.

Shaking his head, he replied, "None. A dragon took my little brother. Then my big brother fell in a slime pit."

The girl sighed. She picked up a leafy branch and walked to the hole. Rudy quickly followed her.

Finn was very surprised to see a girl peering down at him, followed by Rudy, and then a dangling branch. He grabbed onto it, and they pulled him out of the trap. He sat on a rock and looked at his cape. The slime was rolling off the feathers and landing on the grass with a *splat*.

Six Seconds in June

When Defending Your Family
Becomes First Degree Murder

Martin J Coté

The girl told him that the capes were slime-proof. Finn found this fascinating and asked the girl who she was.

"I'm Elia, a trainee dragon tamer from the Willow Clan. You're not from around here, are you?"

Finn and Rudy told her all about the magical storm, the plane, and finding the capes and helmets. Then came the part about the small yellow dragon flying off with their brother.

"Ah, that's Lucca. He's the smallest dragon but also the sneakiest," Elia replied. "My clan's been trying to tame him for years."

On seeing Rudy's and Finn's confused looks, she told them all about the dragon tamers and the dragons of her world. All dragons were capable of being tamed, but some were easier than others. The mischievous ones set up traps to stop the dragon tamers, like the one Finn had fallen into.

Finn scratched his slime-splattered nose and asked her, "Do you know where Jay is?"

"Mischief Mountain." She pointed to the enormous mountain in the distance. "That's where the untamed dragons live. To get your brother back, you have to sneak inside it and follow the three steps to tame Lucca."

Finn and Rudy stared at the giant mountain and gulped. The idea of a mountain filled with untamed dragons sounded scary. But they couldn't leave Jay there. They had to get their brother back!

CHAPTER FIVE

The thought of being stuck with sneaky dragons forever was very scary. But not as scary as the thought of returning home without Jay. Losing him in a faraway land would make their parents very mad.

Finn and Rudy followed Elia toward Mischief Mountain. When they reached the base of it, they craned their necks to look up—it was even scarier and bigger up close.

They peered out from behind a rock and saw two large, scaly dragons guarding the entrance. They were so big that Finn and Rudy trembled at the sight of them.

"Now what?" Finn asked. "We can't just stroll past those two."

"We need to distract them." Elia stared at a pile of leaves and grinned. "I have an idea."

She was an expert at spotting dragon traps. She knew that the pile of leaves was definitely one.

She told Finn and Rudy to gather sticks, which they carefully placed over the leaves to hide them. On top of it, they put a round, tough, pink fruit known as a bonus fruit. This was a dragon's favorite food.

Now, they just needed to coax the dragons over to it. Elia cupped her hands to her mouth and let out an echoing, *"Cooo, coooo, cooooo!"*

Both of the dragon guards twitched their ears and flared their nostrils. The one with spiked, green scales stomped over to the sound, swishing his long tail behind him as he moved.

The children hid behind the rock and watched as the dragon appeared. He took one look at the bonus fruit, licked his lips, then hurried over to it.

The ground opened up. The dragon let out an alarmed growl as he fell into a pit of slithery, slippery weeds.

"Sid, it happened again!" he shouted to the other dragon.

The dragon rolled her eyes and shook her head. She left the entrance unguarded and went to rescue her friend.

Elia, Finn, and Rudy snuck inside the mountain. There were chambers inside with small, glowing bugs glimmering on the rocky walls.

"This way." Elia waved them through one of the rooms.

In front of them was a maze. Only this wasn't like the mazes back home. The walls were made from wriggly, squirming vines. They spotted one of the walls crawl across the ground and settle down in a new spot.

"Lucca's lair is on the other side," Elia told them. "This maze will be full of unwelcome surprises. Don't touch the walls, and watch where you step."

"Let's stick together," Finn said as he prepared himself for the task.

Only, the tricky maze had other ideas. As Rudy followed Finn and Elia along the passageway, long vine arms sprung out from the wall and grabbed him. The entire wall slid through the maze. When it eventually stopped and let go of him, a dizzy Rudy realized he was on the other side.

"Hello? Finn? Elia?" he shouted.

But just then, a tuneless melody sounded from the walls. It echoed through the passageways and gave everyone a headache.

"What's that awful noise?" Finn clasped his hands over his ears. That's when he noticed that Rudy wasn't behind him anymore. "Rudy, where are you?" he tried to shout, but the noise blocked out his voice.

In the commotion, Elia lost her footing and touched one of the walls. Suddenly, a swarm of gooey, sticky bugs appeared and stuck to her cape and helmet.

"Eww! Get off me!" She flicked a bug from her shoulder. But they clumped around her boots, sticking her to the ground. She tried to shake them off, but they flew onto her fingers and stuck them together, too.

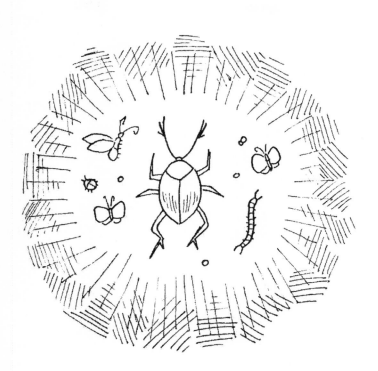

Finn turned to help her, but he didn't see the red circle beneath his foot. As soon as he stepped on it, the ground went wobbly. It was just like walking through an inflatable castle.

He bounced and stumbled along, unable to keep his footing. He was starting to feel very frustrated. He didn't want to be stuck in this annoying maze forever. Something flickered ahead of him, above the maze walls: a bluish-black, shiny feather.

Knowing he needed to overcome this maze to save his brothers, Finn carefully wibbled and wobbled onto shaky feet. Then in one swift movement, he leaped over the bouncy section of floor and went to rescue Elia.

He tried to pry the sticky bugs off her hands. Then they both smacked them off her boots. The pair raced through the maze, weaving past the sliding walls, jumping over colored circles, ducking out of the way of dangling nets, and avoiding any strange-looking cracks and dents.

They followed the feather until they found Rudy standing on tiptoes waving the feather above the maze wall. Finn grabbed his arm, and the three of them carried on, darting, crouching, and swerving at just the right moments.

Soon, they stepped out of the maze into a quiet, damp, moss-covered chamber. Voices sounded in the distance. As they quietly crept along, they spotted Jay perching on a stool made out of rocks.

The yellow dragon was next to him. Although he may have been small for a dragon, he was still ten times the size of the boy. The dragon licked his lips and took a step closer to Jay with a hungry look in his eyes.

CHAPTER SIX

Finn and Rudy were sure the dragon was going to gobble up their brother. They knew they had to work fast to tame the dragon to stop him.

"Follow the three steps," Elia told them. "First, you need to pluck a feather from your cape. Then tickle the dragon under his chin with it."

Finn pulled a feather from his cape and crept toward the dragon. Only, Jay saw him and waved. The dragon turned to see what was going on. As Finn tried to leap forward, Lucca snatched the feather out of his hand. Then the dragon started tickling

Finn with it. Finn couldn't help but laugh—he was very ticklish.

Over the laughter, Elia told Rudy, "Second, you must roll under the dragon without getting squished."

Rudy loved to somersault and tumble, so he thought this would be easy. He snuck around the side of Lucca, who was still distracted with tickling Finn. He did a running roll, but . . . he misjudged and instead of ending up under the dragon, he landed in a water hole. Splash!

While Elia helped pull Rudy out of the water, Finn was able to break free from Lucca's tickling. Elia announced, "Third, a stare-off must be won against the dragon."

Elia, Rudy, and Finn all stared into the dragon's large, amber eyes. Only, Elia let out a loud *achoo!* and couldn't help but blink.

Rudy tried to keep his focus, but an enormous, long-legged insect landed on his T-shirt. He tried to remove it, but it scuttled beneath his cape. He flung off the cape and shook himself to make the insect flee. During this, he had looked away from the dragon.

As the last one left, Finn concentrated extra hard. His eyes felt weary and dry, but he knew he couldn't give up. Out of the corner of his eye, he saw Jay smiling and waving at him. He was about to smile back when Jay stuck out his tongue. As Jay made more silly faces at him, he felt a giggle rising in his throat.

He tried to hold it back, but his little brother was just too funny. Finn burst out laughing, and his eyes were watering so much he blinked.

The dragon shook his head and then prowled toward Jay.

"Noooo!" Finn shouted.

He was certain the dragon meant to hurt Jay now. But then something surprising happened. On reaching Jay, Lucca stuck out his long, rough tongue and tapped his nostril with it.

Jay chuckled and pulled the sides of his mouth with his fingers. The pair exchanged lots of silly faces. Finn, Rudy, and Elia watched on in confusion. As the silliness continued, their puzzled looks turned into smiles. One by one, they joined Jay and Lucca and made their own silly faces.

There was a lot of teeth baring, nose squishing, eye bulging, mouth pulling, and tongue wiggling, which resulted in many belly laughs. They used up all of their energy laughing. Then Lucca nuzzled his head in Jay's lap and made purring sounds. Jay gently patted his scales.

The children realized that the dragon wasn't scary at all. He was actually a very friendly dragon. Finn approached and said, "Um, Lucca, we're sorry we misjudged you, but we really need our brother back."

"Oh," Lucca said sadly. "It's so lonely here by myself." "Can't you play with the other dragons?" Rudy asked. "They're too busy setting up the traps for the dragon tamers. The dragons in the mountain don't want to be tamed, but still, the tamers keep trying."

46

"But you need to be tamed. Otherwise, you cause mayhem by leaving traps everywhere," Elia insisted.

"We only make the traps because we don't want to be tamed." Lucca shook his scaly head. "If we wanted to be, then we'd purposely lose the staring contest. It's impossible to beat a dragon at one unless they choose to let you." "It is?" Elia gasped.

Lucca nodded and sighed. "You humans either try to tame us or run away scared from us. Except for Jay. He didn't hide from me, he waved. That's why I took him."

"I'm sorry you're lonely, but you shouldn't have flown off with our brother like that. We were worried," Finn said.

Lucca thought about this, then replied, "I know. I'm sorry."

Right there in Mischief Mountain, peace was made between the dragon tamers and the dragons. From then on, the dragon tamers would only tame dragons that wanted to be tamed. In exchange, the untamed dragons would stop leaving stinky slime traps across the land.

CHAPTER SEVEN

The brothers spent the rest of the day playing with their new friends. They chased each other through the maze, careful to avoid the slime pits; they had a make-the-silliest-face contest — Elia judged it and chose Lucca as the winner; and they took turns flying across the land on the dragon's back.

When it was Jay's turn, both he and Lucca arrived with ice-cream-covered mouths. It turned out that dragons loved ice cream just as much as humans did.

Finn noticed that the fluffy clouds were fading in the sky. He pointed up at them and told his brothers that they better leave before there were no magical clouds left.

Jay hugged Lucca, made one last silly face at him, then passed him a sticky sweet out of his pocket.

Rudy peeled two stickers from his T-shirt. He passed the dragon sticker to Lucca and the mountain sticker to Elia to remember the boys by. Lucca was so pleased with his gift that he almost set fire to it—by accident, of course. Luckily, the embers missed the sticker and hit one of Rudy's cape feathers and sizzled out.

They waved goodbye to Elia and Lucca and walked back to the plane. There, they took off their capes and helmets and put them back in the chest. They climbed into the plane and strapped themselves in. Finn pressed the controls and steered them up into the clouds.

They landed with a *thud*.

All three hurried out of the plane and looked around them. They were back in their sunny front yard.

As Rudy looked at the plane, he asked, "Um, how do we explain the plane to Mom and Dad?"

Finn replied, "I don't know. We can't just leave it here. There has to be a way to do something." The brothers walked around the plane trying to find a way to change it back into a chalk drawing.

That's when Rudy spotted a small, shiny button on the right wing. He waved his brothers over and pointed at it.

"What do you think it does?" Finn asked.

"Don't know." Rudy shrugged. "Let's find out."

Jay giggled as he hovered his hand above the button. Rudy pressed his hand over Jay's. Then they both looked at Finn.

"Here goes nothing," Finn whispered as he pressed his hand over Rudy's.

On the count of three, they moved their hands in unison and pressed the button.

There was a *zzzziiip* sound. In the blink of an eye, the plane disappeared. Finn touched the spot where it had been to see if it was invisible . . . but he just gripped air. Rudy peered up at the clear, blue sky to see if it had flown away . . . but it wasn't there either.

Jay looked at the ground and excitedly jumped up and down on bare feet. He wiggled his finger toward the pavement.

There on the ground was the plane. Only it was now a teeny, tiny, miniature version.

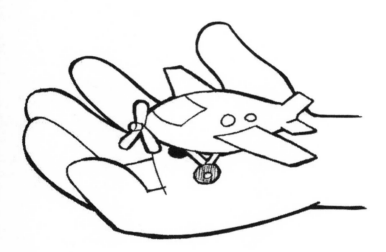

Finn scooped it up in his palm and inspected it, amazed at how small it had become. He went to put it in one of his pockets, but they were already full of chalk.

"My pocket's empty," Rudy said. He grabbed the plane from his brother. "Don't lose it. You lose everything." Finn glared at him.

"Do not," he grunted, patting his pocket

"You lost that toy car Grandma bought you."

"Did not. Jay took it."

Jay didn't hear his name being mentioned. He was already running into the house. As the sweet scent of ice cream wafted out the door, Finn and Rudy exchanged grins.

They hurried after their brother.

Deep in Rudy's pocket, next to an orange paperclip and a green star sticker that had lost its stick, the miniature plane was ready and waiting for the next magical adventure.

Made in United States
Troutdale, OR
11/25/2024

25268005R00039